BRAIN DRAIN BABY

OTHER BOOKS IN THE NIGHTMARE CLUB SERIES

THE NIGHTMARE CLUB

BRAIN DRAIN BABY

BY

ANNIE GRAVES

ILLUSTRATED BY
GLENN McELHINNEY

Little Island

Brain Drain Baby
First published in 2015 by
Little Island Books
7 Kenilworth Park
Dublin 6W, Ireland

Illustrations © Glenn McElhinney 2015
except house on front cover and p ii, by Jacktoon

ISBN: 978-1-910411-35-3

A British Library Cataloguing in Publication record
for this book is available from the British Library

Book design by Fidelma Slattery

Typeset in Trebuchet MS by Vincent Connare and October Crow by
Chad Savage. Cover title typeface also used in interior: Remnant by
Chris Au, www.chrisau-design.co.uk

Printed in Poland by Drukarnia Skleniarz

Little Island receives financial assistance from the Arts Council/An
Chomhairle Ealaíon and from the Arts Council of Northern Ireland

Supported by
The National Lottery®
through the Arts Council of Northern Ireland

10 9 8 7 6 5 4 3 2 1

To all older brothers and sisters —
because you understand

Annie Graves is twelve years old, and she has no intention of ever growing up. She is, conveniently, an orphan, and lives at an undisclosed address in the Glasnevin area of Dublin with her pet toad, Much Misunderstood, and a small black kitten, Hugh Shalby Nameless.

You needn't think she goes to school — pah! — or has anything as predictable as brothers and sisters or anything as dull as hobbies, but let's just say she keeps a large saucepan on the stove.

This is not her first book. She has written ten so far, none of which is her first.

Publisher's note: We did try to take a picture of Annie, but her face just kept fading away. We have sent our camera for investigation.

THANK YOU!

Yeah, well, I'm not all that polite, so saying thank you is very boring for me. But my publishers tell me I have to thank this Dave Rudden guy. For some unknown reason. He's some writer dude they are friends with. Nothing to do with this book. Absolutely nothing. But, hey, Dave, thanks for being a writer dude that the people at Little Island like.

(WILL THAT DO, PUBLISHERS?)

This is me, Annie Graves, author extraordinaire. (That's French, not a spelling mistake.)

Look, just so you know, this whole Nightmare Club thing was my idea.

It's a sleepover, and everyone has to tell a story. That's how the Nightmare Club works. And it'd better be a scary one, or you're out. Home you go.

And only the scariest
stories are good enough for
the Nightmare Club. That's my
rule. I make the rules around here because
I'm in charge.

This is Barry's story.

He's a strange boy, Barry.

A bit confused. A bit forgetful.

A bit ... missing.

Barry stared at us with eyes as wide and bright and round as frightened moons.

'Did you know,' he said in a scared little voice, 'that babies don't *know anything*?'

'Yes,' said Laura.

'Yeah,' said Colm.

'Of course,' I said. 'So?'

Barry's wide eyes narrowed. 'What do you mean *so*? Isn't that weird? Isn't that *creepy*?'

We stared at him.

'They don't know *anything*!' he shouted. '*Nothing* at all!'

Barry hadn't been in the Nightmare Club for very long. He didn't know we were tough. We don't scare easy, and it takes a *lot* to frighten *me*.

Babies were not going to cut it, I thought, panning the torch around the group, and by the looks on everyone else's faces I wasn't the only one.

'So what?' Colm said. His mum had just brought home a little brother and I was prepared to let him be the Nightmare Club's baby expert.

(I don't like babies. They're weird, and they don't say anything clever, and they look like half-cooked bread rolls. I suppose I was a baby once, but the less I think about it the better.)

'Of course babies don't know anything,' Colm continued, 'cos they're only new and stuff. They haven't learned anything yet. That's not weird. That's just a fact. Facts aren't scary. They're just *facts*.'

'Yeah, you think that,' Barry said, and
his hands were drumming on his knees as
if he was going to tell us a great secret,
'but I know different.'

And this was the story that he told us.

I was an only child. I liked being an only child.

I was the youngest.

And I was the oldest.

I got the whole back seat of the car all to myself.

If I found sweets in the cupboard I didn't have to wonder who they were for — and I didn't have to share.

Life was good.

AND THEN

SHE CAME.

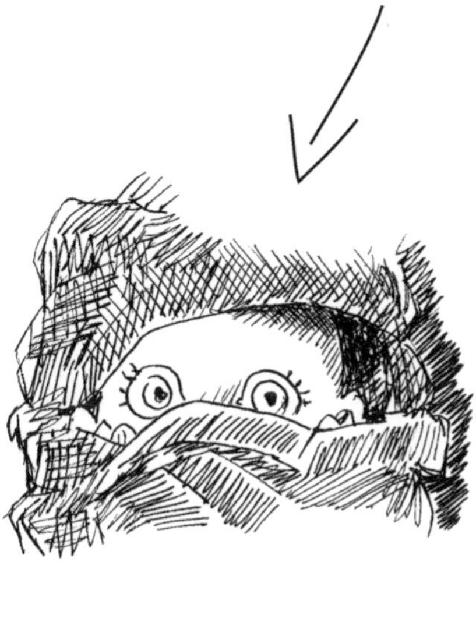

I mean, I knew it was going to happen.

Mum spent nine months getting big and waddly, and then one day she went to the hospital and when she came back she had a baby with her.

All wrapped up in pink cloth until all you could see were big blue eyes peeking out. Like a mole. Like a robber in a story with their face hidden.

Carried in the front door like she owned the place.

And it wasn't long before she did.

I am a professional aunt-pleaser. My mum
has *loads* of sisters. And they're not a
tough crowd. Most times all I have to do
is walk through the kitchen and next
thing you know there is a FIVE EURO
NOTE in my hand.

It's a *career*, aunt-pleasing, and I take it
very seriously.

But once the baby came home? Well.
Suddenly it was 'my little princess' this,
and 'oh my pink little star' that.

'If she's a princess,' I'd say to myself,
just loud enough for only me to hear,
'that'd make me a prince. And princes
are better.'

I'd try and avoid her when I could.

Playing football outside, taking Francis
(our tiny fluff-ball dog) for walks. I even
started working hard at school.

I had a test about Egypt coming up.

I had to know the capital city.

I had to know things about the pyramids.

I had to know the money they used.

I had to know what temperature it got to in summer and what temperature it got to in winter.

Normally I hate studying, but when the choice is to do homework or to listen to people coo over a little smushface in pink, then I'm going to study.

Finally Mum and Dad notice that I'm not around.

They bring me down so I can be *properly acquainted with the new arrival.* So I sit, and I stare.

And it stares back.

Mum's eyes are brown — the colour of chocolate.

Dad's eyes (and mine) are the brown of new pennies.

But the baby's were blue. Big and blue and staring at me. She had no expression at all on her face, and after a few seconds I began to feel a bit weird.

'What does it do?' I said.

Mum laughed. 'It doesn't *do* anything,'
she said. 'It's a baby. Babies are brand
new. They don't know how to do
anything. They're like pages with nothing
written on them.'

It looked a little like a pink snowman, just one big ball for its head smushed onto another bigger ball for its body.

Its fingers were like scrunchy little sausages and it had no hair at all on its head.

And that's when I saw it.

I couldn't believe it.

SHE
WINKED!

'She just …' I said in horror. 'She …'

'She what?' Mum said.

The baby continued to stare at me, her eyes bright and blue and strange.

There was a gleam to them, as if they were reflecting a light I couldn't see, a light from somewhere very far away.

WOM.
WOM.
WOM.

What was that sound?

Mum was saying something but I wasn't listening.

All I could do was stare at my little sister's eyes.

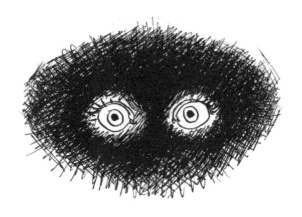

The sound grew louder until there wasn't anything else. Just me, and blue eyes, and —

WOM.

WOM.

W—

'BARRY!'

I jumped half-
out of my
skin. 'What?'

Mum was
pointing upstairs.
'Go to bed.'

I went to bed.

The next day the teacher came around
and put sheets of paper in front of us.
We were to write everything we
remembered about Egypt. And I sat,
pencil in hand, and I stared at that sheet
for the whole time until the bell rang,
and nothing came out.

I had forgotten *everything*.

I know, I know — maybe I just forgot!
(Not that I'll ever forget the look on my
teacher's face when I handed her a blank
sheet of paper.)

But then I came home, and when we were sitting at dinner (not going to forget the looks on my parents' faces when they found out about the test either), I happened to look over at the little *princess*.

She was staring back at me. Like she was always staring at me. Her chubby little sausage fingers were moving around and around on the top of her blanket, like she was *drawing* something. But babies can't draw, right? They can't do *anything*.

I looked closer, tried to follow what she was drawing, and then I froze with shock. I knew what she was drawing. I recognised the shape.

IT
WAS A
PYRAMID
!!!!!!!!!!!!!!!!!!!!

How did she know what a pyramid was? She was a baby! How could she have ...

And then it struck me. How *did* babies learn things? Maybe she had — *hypnotised* me or something, with her weird baby smushface, and those terrible blue eyes, and dragged me in, and *stolen knowledge out of my head*. That was why I couldn't remember anything about Egypt, even though I had studied it all night.

The baby looked at me with its big blue eyes.

They were like blank pages. That was what Mum had said. I knew what was going on. The baby wanted all the stuff in my head to fill it up.

And that's when I heard it again.

WOM.

Coming from that ice-blue stare.

WOM.

Wanting me to stare back.

WOM.

Wanting to *steal* all the stuff in my head.

WOM.

So that was it. My little sister, the little smushface baby invader of my home, was some kind of memory stealer. A mind vampire. A brain drainer.

This time it had only been schoolwork. What would happen the next time? Would she take my hard-won knowledge of cartoons?

I became more and more worried with each day.

'Mum, can I have my favourite for dinner tonight?'

(My favourite is mashed potato with cheese and bacon. I am constantly surprised it is not everyone's favourite.)

Mum was sitting on the couch, absently patting Francis's fluffy head. 'What?'

'My favourite,' I repeated. 'Mashed potato with bacon and cheese.'

'Potatoes,' she repeated — slowly, as if she had never heard the word before. 'Are those the long orange ones?'

'Mum, that's carrots.'

'Right,' Mum said. 'Carrots. Sorry. Potatoes are the ones you have to fish out of the ocean.'

'No, Mum!' I nearly shouted. 'That's fish!'

'Right,' Mum said again. 'Sorry. I'm just not with it today.'

'Have you seen my keys?' Dad said, as he tramped around the living room.

'Over there,' Mum said, pointing at the hook where Dad *always* kept his keys.

'Ah, of course,' Dad responded with a laugh. 'I'll forget my own head next!'

THIS HAD **TO STOP.**

'What am I going to do, Francis?' I said.

'Wuff,' said Francis sleepily.

Francis is very old and looks like a cloud with currants for eyes. He doesn't seem to worry about much.

'Easy for you to say,' I muttered. 'You've got nothing in your head to steal.'

And then it hit me.

The baby was sucking all the clever stuff
out of people's heads. Stuff they needed
for tests and being parents. And the
more it took, the smarter it was getting.
Maybe soon nobody would be safe.

But what if I gave it something else to
suck on instead? Something it mightn't
like the taste of so much?

It took a lot of courage to go downstairs to the sitting room. I walked so slowly even Francis outpaced me.

'Your sister's napping,' Mum said when I went through the kitchen. 'Keep an eye on her while I ...' She paused. '... do the thing. The ... something something.'

'Make dinner?' I suggested.

'Yes,' Mum said. 'That was it. Thanks.'

No problem, Mum. I'll keep an eye on her all right.

I crept into the
room. The baby was
snoozing in its high chair,
but I didn't trust that. I scooped
Francis up in my arms and tucked him a
little into my coat so you couldn't see
him. He snuffled and
guffled sleepily.

'Wuff,' he said, half
to himself. I
completely
agreed.

Suddenly the baby's eyes opened.

It was like being caught under a floodlight.

They gleamed at me —

big and blue

and

HUNGRY.

WOM.

There it was.

WOM.

The sound of the stare. Calling me.
Trying to hypnotise me.

I took a step forward — I couldn't help it.
It was like little strings were dragging
me. I took another. Another.

What would I lose this time? What would
the little smushface take from me?

Another step. I was looking at the television, at the floor, at anything but her. It was harder and harder with each step I took. My head kept trying to turn.

Closer. Closer. *Closer.*

And then I swung Francis up like a shield,
and he met the baby's gaze full-on.

Eat this, I thought.

'Wuff,' said Francis.

The drag of her eyes abruptly stopped.

The invisible strings surrounding me were cut.

I jumped backwards and let Francis down to wuffle his way into the corner.

Mum's voice called out through the door. 'Dinner's ready!'

After that — well, everything went back to normal. I didn't hear the *wom wom* of her stare anymore and the teacher gave us another test and I got ten out of ten on it. So everything worked out pretty well.

But still. Babies. *Ugh*.

We all stared at Barry.

He had a big proud smile on his face, as if he had defeated the Seven Deadly Vampires of Crossmaglen or something.

(He hadn't. I had. I'll tell you about that some day.)

'That,' Colm said, 'is gross. You let a dog lick your little sister's face? Gross.'

'It wasn't *gross*,' Barry said a little huffily. 'It was necessary. I wasn't losing any more brainstuff to a little baby.'

'I don't know,' I said. 'It's not exactly Nightmare Club material.'

'Well, I'm not finished,' Barry said. 'Thing is, that was a while ago. My little sister just said her first word last week.'

'Oh,' Colm said, 'was it Egypt?'

'No,' Barry said.

'IT WAS WUFF!'

WWW.THENIGHTMARECLUB.COM